Raccoon

Published in the United States of America by Cherry Lake Publishing
Ann Arbor, Michigan
www.cherrylakepublishing.com

Reading Adviser: Marla Conn MS, Ed., Literacy specialist, Read-Ability, Inc.
Book Design: Jennifer Wahi
Illustrator: Jeff Bane

Photo Credits: © Dennis Jacobsen / Shutterstock.com, 5; © Ondrej Prosicky / Shutterstock.com, 7; © worldswildlifewonders / Shutterstock.com, 9; © Volodymyr Burdiak / Shutterstock.com, 11; © Debbie Steinhausser / Shutterstock.com, 13; © Edwin Butter / Shutterstock.com, 15; © kelly999 / Shutterstock.com, 17; © Geoffrey Kuchera / Shutterstock.com, 19; © FotoRequest / Shutterstock.com, 21; © penphoto / Shutterstock.com, 23; © Ozerina Anna 2-3, 24; Cover, 1, 8, 16, 20, Jeff Bane

Library of Congress Cataloging-in-Publication Data

Names: Loh-Hagan, Virginia, author.
Title: Raccoon / by Virginia Loh-Hagan.
Description: Ann Arbor : Cherry Lake Publishing, 2017. | Series: My favorite
    animal | Audience: Grade K to grade 3. | Includes index.
Identifiers: LCCN 2017000950| ISBN 9781634728409 (hardcover) | ISBN
    9781534100183 (pbk.) | ISBN 9781634729291 (pdf) | ISBN 9781534101074
    (hosted ebook)
Subjects: LCSH: Raccoon--Juvenile literature.
Classification: LCC QL737.C26 L63 2017 | DDC 599.76/32--dc23
LC record available at https://lccn.loc.gov/2017000950

Printed in the United States of America
Corporate Graphics

table of contents

About the author: Dr. Virginia Loh-Hagan is an author, university professor, former classroom teacher, and curriculum designer. Her dog Woody has a black mask, just like raccoons. She lives in San Diego with her very tall husband and very naughty dogs. To learn more about her, visit www.virginialoh.com.

About the illustrator: Jeff Bane and his two business partners own a studio along the American River in Folsom, California, home of the 1849 Gold Rush. When Jeff's not sketching or illustrating for clients, he's either swimming or kayaking in the river to relax.

looks

Raccoons have a mostly white face. There are circles of black fur around each eye. This helps them see at night. It looks like they're wearing a mask.

They weigh about 15 pounds (7 kilograms). They have a bushy tail. Their tail has rings. The rings are black and white.

What can you do with your hands?

They have special front paws. Their paws have five toes. The paws are like hands. They open things. They **sense** things. Raccoons can move their paws quickly.

Raccoons live in North America. They live in Europe. They live in Japan. They live in woods. They live in mountains. They live by water.

Some raccoons live in cities.
They live in gardens and parks.

Raccoons will eat almost anything. They eat bugs. They eat fish and eggs. They eat small animals. They eat fruits and nuts.

How does hunting at night help raccoons?

Raccoons are active at night. They hunt at night. They eat at night. They sleep during the day.

Raccoons pick up food. They look at it. They rub it. They remove parts they don't want. If they're near water, they wash their food.

776

19

Why might a raccoon want to swim?

Raccoons spend much of their time in trees. They can climb fast. Raccoons also swim well. They can hold their breath under water.

Raccoons eat a lot in spring and summer. They **store** fat. They sleep for weeks at a time in winter. They live off the stored body fat.

glossary

sense (SENS) to feel

store (STOR) to build up, to save

index